W9-ATU-615

Power Chord

Power Chord

Ted Staunton

orca currents

ORCA BOOK PUBLISHERS

FIC
STA

Library and Archives Canada Cataloguing in Publication

Staunton, Ted, 1956-
Power chord / Ted Staunton.
(Orca currents)

Issued also in electronic format.
ISBN 978-1-55469-904-9 (bound).--ISBN 978-1-55469-903-2 (pbk.)

I. Title. II. Series: Orca currents
PS8587.T334P69 2011   JC813'.54   C2011-903427-1

First published in the United States, 2011
Library of Congress Control Number: 2011929395

Summary: Fourteen-year-old Ace starts a band and learns a tough
lesson about plagiarism.

*Orca Book Publishers is dedicated to preserving the environment and has printed this
book on paper certified by the Forest Stewardship Council®.*

Orca Book Publishers gratefully acknowledges the support for its
publishing programs provided by the following agencies: the Government
of Canada through the Canada Book Fund and the Canada Council for the Arts,
and the Province of British Columbia through the BC Arts Council
and the Book Publishing Tax Credit.

Cover photography by First Light

ORCA BOOK PUBLISHERS   ORCA BOOK PUBLISHERS
PO Box 5626, Stn. B   PO Box 468
Victoria, BC Canada   Custer, WA USA
v8R 6s4   98240-0468

www.orcabook.com
Printed and bound in Canada.

14 13 12 11 • 4 3 2 1

Thanks to Liz, Kim, Bernice, Tabitha, Sue, Florence, Roma, Lindsay and Daniel, for great suggestions, and to my son Will, for great music.

Chapter One

Denny is yelling, but I can't hear his words. Onstage, Twisted Hazard has just ripped their last chord. It's still bouncing around the gym.

"What?" I yell back. I pull the tissue out of my ears. I always take tissue to Battle of the Bands.

"*I got a great idea*," Denny yells.

Denny gets lots of ideas. His last one called for coconuts, shaving cream and our math teacher's car. If this is a *great* idea, it'll be the first time he's ever had one.

"What is it?" I say.

Denny says, "We hafta start a band."

"What for?"

"What *for*?" Denny waves at the stage. The Hazard bass player is a hobbit in red plaid pajama pants. He's talking to two girls in amazingly tight jeans. The lead singer looks too young to stay out after the streetlights come on, plus he's in chess club. Three girls, one very hot, are chatting with him. The drummer has glasses and is wearing flood pants. He's handing his snare and a cymbal to two girls in grade *ten*. One of them is his sister, but still.

"Look at those guys," Denny says. "Imagine how we'd do."

I hate to admit it, but maybe Denny has a point. Those guys are in grade nine, and we're in grade nine. They are nerds, and yet those girls are all over them.

We're not nerds—even if Denny's ears do stick out—but we're invisible to girls. There are girls all around us, in cool shapes and sizes and smells. They don't help *us* with anything, except maybe give us something to stare at.

Maybe a band is the answer. I bet playing in a band is easier than playing basketball, especially for someone my size. There's a problem though.

"Uh, Den," I say, "don't you have to play music to be in a band?"

Up onstage, the next group is plugging in. It's No Money Down. The guitar players are in my English class.

"Well, *duh*," Denny says. He's patting his pockets. He pulls out his cell and flips it open. "No problem. You've got that stuff at your house."

There is a bass and a guitar at my place. I fool around on them a little.

Denny says, "And I play guitar and sing."

Denny did take some guitar lessons a couple of years back.

"Since when do you sing?" I ask. In between ideas, Denny has been known to lie.

"Me?" he says. "I sing great. I was in that choir, remember?"

I make a face and say, "So was I, Den. That was grade four."

Denny says, "Yeah, well, I sing all the time at home. While I'm playing guitar. I just don't do it around other people. Anyway, it's your band style that counts."

"Band style?" I say.

Denny says, "Yeah. You know, your look, your attitude. That stuff. Like, notice how cool bands never smile in pictures? Anyway, most of them don't even play, they fake along to their records."

"How do you know?" I ask.

Denny shrugs. "Everybody knows that."

"One problem, Den," I say, "we won't have any records to fake to."

Denny is too busy texting to answer.

How did we end up talking about starting a band? Really, we only came to see who was around. And to look at girls and make jokes about them we don't really mean. Soon we'll probably yell and fake wrestle with some other guys. Later we'll walk back to my place to watch downloads of *Python Pit 6* and *Facemelt* and laugh at them. I mean, you have to do *something* on a Friday night.

Up onstage, some goof from the student government introduces No Money Down. One of the guitar players hits a power chord behind him. Everybody is crowding the stage around them. Girls are crowding the stage around them.

I look at the two guys from English. They look the same as they do in English, only they don't. They have sweet guitars that I don't know the make of. Lights are shining on them, and everybody is watching. They're trying to look cool, but you can tell they want to giggle like little kids.

Do I want that? Yes I do. I turn to Denny and say, "Let's do it."

"Wait." He's still texting.

"Who are you texting anyway?" I ask.

"I'm not texting." Denny looks up and grins his big maniac grin. "I'm tweeting."

"What?" I say. "Since when are you on Twitter?"

"Since today. Look, I just told the world." He holds up his phone as No Money Down stomp off their first song. On the screen it reads: **Hot new band**

startup 4 u. dr. d & ace will rule. watch for more later.

"Let's do it, Ace," Denny says.

"Props." We bump fists. I'm in.

Chapter Two

We decide the first thing we need to do is find a drummer. We start at three on Saturday afternoon. We're not what you call early risers.

"We'll get Pigpen," Denny says to me on the phone.

"I didn't know Pig played drums," I say.

"His older brother has drums. He was in that band, remember, when we were in grade eight."

I do remember. They were pretty good, even though at the time, I said they sucked.

"His brother plays drums, but that doesn't mean Pig does," I say.

"I heard Pig tapping pencils in study hall," Denny says. "He's great."

We meet at the bus stop. Pig lives a ways from us. When the bus arrives, Denny insists we sneak on the back doors as other people get off. Not many people get off on a Saturday.

Right away, the driver calls, "You in the green hoodie!"

Denny looks around as if he's not wearing a green hoodie. He's also grinning.

"And your buddy," calls the driver. "No free rides. Get up here. Pay your fares or get off."

Everyone stares at us, which I don't like. Denny grins bigger than ever. We shuffle up front, digging in our pockets for cash.

It's a seven-stop ride. When we get to Pigpen's house and ring the bell, his mom answers. Denny blathers all over her, the way he always does with adults. I wait. Actually she is pretty nice.

"Jared!" she calls down to the basement. Jared is Pigpen's real name. "Friends!" She sends us downstairs.

Pigpen is not exactly a friend of ours, but we knew him in grade three. Then his family moved. We met him again this year when we all started at the same high school. His nickname is kind of a joke, because he's a neat freak. He has a buzz cut and always tucks in his shirt. His jeans are pressed. Even his locker is organized. It's spooky.

When we get downstairs, Pigpen is polishing a pair of black combat boots.

I wonder if he's a closet punker. Sure enough, a drum kit is set up in the corner.

Denny makes his pitch. Pig listens, then nods. "Okay," he says.

Pig isn't a talker. He could have been in silent movies. Denny is a talker. In fact Denny is a motormouth. I can be a talker with my friends, but not around adults.

"Cool," says Denny.

There are more props all round. I notice Pig is wearing latex gloves to keep his hands clean as he polishes.

Denny says, "I'll bring over my Tely, and Ace has got a bass and amp and—"

"Can't," says Pig.

"Huh?" we say.

"Can't." Pig dabs more polish on a boot. Then he says, "Mom won't let us. Too loud. Said New Teeth made her grind her own." New Teeth had been the name of Pig's brother's band.

"But the drums are here," I say.

"Gotta move 'em," Pig says. He starts buffing the toe of a boot with a brush. "My brother won't care. He's away at school till Christmas. We can use his microphone too."

"There's no room at my place," says Denny. He's right. That leaves us with my place. They both look at me.

I sigh. "I'll have to ask my mom."

"So call her," Denny says.

"She said not to call unless there's a disaster. She's showing a house." Mom sells real estate. She says the market is slow.

"Then let's take everything over. How can she say no?"

"She can say no lots of ways, Den," I say. "I'll ask when she gets home."

Denny grabs the hi-hat anyway. The pedal clunks off on his foot. "Ow, Jee—" He cuts off. Pig's mom is upstairs.

"So let's go," I say.

Denny is limp-hopping around the room.

"Call me," Pig says.

"Aren't you coming?" Denny looks back at him, still limp-hopping.

Pig picks up an unpolished boot and nods at it.

"Later," I say.

"Later."

Chapter Three

We're out of cash, so Denny and I walk the seven stops back to my house.

Denny says, "Pig didn't even want to come with us." He shakes his head in amazement.

"He was busy, Den," I say.

"Yeah, see those boots? What was that about?"

I shrug. "Maybe he's a professional grape stomper."

Denny says, "Don't you wear hip waders for that?"

My mom isn't home when we get back to my place. We get snacks. Archie, our cat, pads in and stretches. I give him a snack too.

"Let's check out the stuff," says Denny, as if we haven't a million times before.

We haul everything out from under the basement stairs. There's a microphone stand, a Yorkville bass amp, two guitar cases and a cardboard box. All of it looks pretty battered. Inside the cases are a Squier electric bass and a Cort acoustic guitar with a pickup. I know there are straps, patch cords, a couple of picks, and an electronic tuner with no battery tucked in there too. When you open the cases they let out a whiff of wood polish and plastic, cigarette smoke and beer. The bass case also smells of cat pee. Arch once took a leak in there. It doesn't matter. I like it. It reminds me of Chuck.

Chuck is the owner of all this stuff. He was a boyfriend of Mom's when I was eleven or twelve. Chuck was a goof, but in a good way. I liked him. I think Mom did too, but she said he had "reliability issues."

When Chuck wasn't driving a truck, he played in a band called Razorburn. He said he was only driving truck until his music took off.

Mom said the truck would take off before the music did. She was right.

Inside the cardboard box is a pile of leftover copies of Razorburn's CD, *Mullet Over.* I haven't listened to it in a million years.

Denny is trying to tune the guitar. He gives up and strums. It's not music, but it gets your attention.

"Power chord," says Denny. "See what I'm doing?"

"Mangling the guitar," I say. We hear the door open upstairs.

"Hi," Mom calls.

"We're down here," I call back.

There are footsteps, and then Mom's feet and legs appear on the stairs. I spend a lot of time in the basement. I always like how people on stairs seem to sprout magically in front of you. Mom is wearing her house-showing pantsuit. Mom looks at all the gear spread out. She raises an eyebrow.

"Ask her," Den hisses. "Go on, ask her."

There are reasons I shouldn't ask her. I am supposed to be getting better marks. I am supposed to be looking for a part-time job. I am supposed to be more reliable. Thanks to Chuck, I don't think Mom thinks *reliable* and *music* go together.

On the other hand, Denny and Pig need this too. And getting out this stuff reminds me of how Chuck showed me chords and bits from songs. I liked that. Chuck said I was good too. Above all, there are girls everywhere who don't know I exist, but who soon will—if I ask. I ask.

"We want to start a band. Can we practice here?"

Denny takes a running step off the carpet. He slides toward my mom on his knees across the patch of lino. It's a good rock-and-roll move, actually. He stops in front of her and looks up, his hands together, begging, "Please Mrs. C, please?"

Mom looks from him to me. I am trying to look hardworking and reliable.

Her mouth twitches. She says, "This is going to cost you straight Bs, minimum, on your next report card."

Denny starts tweeting.

Chapter Four

Mom invites Denny to stay for supper, but he has to go. She asks me to make salad while she cooks spaghetti. I start by looking in the junk drawer. "Do we have any batteries?"

"What size?" Mom asks. She's running water to fill a saucepan.

"I don't know," I say, "The square ones."

"Nine-volt," Mom says. "I think there's one. What do you need it for?"

Man. Already she's piling on questions. I say, "The guitar tuner thingy."

"Look in the computer desk." She passes me the knife and cutting board. "After you make salad."

Instead, I look in the computer desk right away. I can't find it.

By now, Mom is browning ground beef in the fry pan. She has stacked the salad vegetables beside the cutting board. "Who else is going to be in the band?"

I say, "Pigpe...Jared."

Mom says, "Really? Jared from grade school?" She turns to look at me.

"Uh-huh."

"That's nice," she says. "I haven't seen Jared in ages. What does he play?"

"Drums." I tear off chunks of lettuce to wash. Will the questions never end?

"Anybody else?" she asks.

"No," I say.

Mom nods and says, "What are you going to call yourselves?"

I turn off the tap. "We haven't decided. Either Green Day or the Beatles."

"All right, smart guy," she says as she takes spaghetti down from the cupboard. "Just..."

"What?" I start chopping carrots, ready for the lecture.

"Never mind," Mom says. She tells me about the people interested in the house instead.

After supper I hit Facebook and try to line up the evening. It is Saturday night, after all. For way too long I write on walls and don't get anything back. Where is everybody?

Finally, Denny writes back and asks if I want to go to Rock 'N Bowl. I'm a bad bowler, but I like Rock 'N Bowl. You don't tell people you like

Rock 'N Bowl though. It sounds lame.
I message back **better than death** and
ask Mom if she'll drive us.

There's an hour to kill before
we pick up Denny. I go down to the
basement and open the guitar cases.
I look at the instruments, nestled in
plush. They are full of music I want to
get at. I remember Chuck showing me
chords and a bass pattern for playing
blues. The guitar had felt big as an army
tank. Now it feels light—and hard, for
something so curvy-looking. I pluck the
strings softly. I don't want Mom to hear.
I also don't know what it's supposed to
sound like.

I take the neck in my left hand and
press down on the littlest string with a
finger. It's tougher than it looks. In fact, it
hurts a little. I pluck with the pick. *Cluk*.
I press harder. Now I get a twang. I stop
the sound with my hand. I remember a
chord Chuck showed me, a G, I think.

Anyway, it's the one where you reach across with two fingers to the two thickest strings. It's tough tucking my little finger in behind. I try a quiet strum.

Yuck. I need that tuner.

I put the guitar down and pick up the bass. It's heavy, and the balance is different. After the guitar, the neck is like a tree. The strings feel thick as snakes. They push back under my fingers, vibrating through me when I pluck them. Cool.

I have to take the next step, even if I'm not in tune. I have to hear the sound, the real sound. It's time for power. I plug the patch cord into the amp and the bass. I flip the power switch. A red light pops on, and the amp starts to hum. I feel my whole body hum with it. I set the volume down low and try again. The strings slither under my fingers. The sound vibrates right into my gut, like it's the center of the Earth.

All at once I can see myself on a stage with Pig and Denny. I feel music swirling all around us, loud music. I see bright lights, and beyond the lights are faces and waving arms. *I want that.* I want it to be me you hear at Rock 'N Bowl, especially if you are a girl.

I start fake singing at the empty microphone stand. I blump at the bass like an idiot. Already my fingers hurt. I close my eyes and make a rock singer face. When I open them, Mom has sprouted on the stairs. I freeze in mid-*blump.*

"Sorry," she says. "I thought you might want this." She's holding a battery.

I say, "Oh. Yeah. Thanks." I can feel my face turn the color of spaghetti sauce. This is worse than being caught on certain websites. I take off the bass, then grab the tuner from the case. "Where was it?" I ask.

Mom smiles. "In the kitchen drawer."

"Oh. I'll just—" I'm fumbling so hard I can't get the tuner open.

"Let me try," Mom says. She takes the tuner. She opens the back and hooks in the battery. She presses the button. Bingo. "Remember how to use it?"

I nod.

"Good," she says. "Didn't Chuck write out some things to get you started?"

"Oh yeahhh…," I say. My face is cooling off. I look in the guitar case. There are pages with writing in pen. One says *How to Tune*. Another has chord charts. I remember practicing making the chords. Another sheet has bass patterns for songs marked on it. There's "Smoke on the Water" and "Sunshine of Your Love." I remember Chuck showing me those. They were cool.

Then I think of something. "Is it, like, okay to—"

"To use Chuck's things?" Mom smiles. "I think so," she says. "In fact, I think he'd like it. Besides, he'd have been back if anything had been important." Her voice changes, and her smile fades.

"Okay," I say. "I thought that since he used to show me stuff…"

She smiles again. "You're right, he did. He was good that way."

"Maybe he forgot it," I say.

Now she laughs. "I wouldn't be surprised. Forgetful was a way of life for Chuck. Remember the time he used two tins of Archie's food by mistake in the—"

Now I laugh and say, "Yeah, and we all had to go out for dinner."

Mom stops laughing. "And I paid. No, Chuck did pay. I shouldn't be so hard on him. He was a nice guy…" Mom sighs and looks at me now. "I'm glad you're giving this a try. Focus is good. But remember your promises, Davey."

David is my real name. Everybody calls me Ace because when I get asked about marks, I always sarcastically say, "A's." Everyone but Mom thinks it's funny. Now I nod my head. "I know," I say.

"Good. We should get going in ten minutes."

I turn off the amp. Mom starts back up the stairs. "Cat food." I hear her chuckle. She vanishes a step at a time.

Chapter Five

"How long till the next bus?" I ask.

Pigpen shrugs. Denny is busy tweeting: **nmbr1 rd. trip w/drums. need rdies nxt time 4 help. R U up 4 it girls?**

We're at the bus stop near Pig's house. It's Tuesday after school, and it's hot for late September. I'm sweating and thirsty because we're carrying the whole drum kit. Also, the fingertips of my left hand are sore.

I've tuned the instruments that are waiting at my house, and I've been practicing. I don't tell Pig and Denny. I want to surprise them with how good I am. Instead I say, "We could have waited till tomorrow. My mom could've given us a ride."

"Rock and roll doesn't wait, Ace." Denny snaps his cell shut. "And Pig's mom wanted the stuff out."

"It was only until tomorrow," I say.

"Who cares?" Denny says. "It's cool. Anyway, it's like free advertising for the band. People will remember us: *I used to see them carrying their drums down the street.*"

This could be true. We're hard to miss. The drums take up a lot of sidewalk. I've got the bass drum, pedal and a cymbal stand. Denny's got the toms, the snare and stand. Sticks are poking out of his back pocket. Pig, the biggest of us, has the cymbals, a stand, the hi-hat stand and another set of sticks. How did he end up carrying so little?

"What we really need," Denny goes on, "are band T-shirts. If we were wearing them, everybody would know who we are and remember when they hear us."

"The T-shirts would be blank, Den," I say. "We don't have a name."

"*Oh yeahhhhh*," Denny says. "Okay, I think we should be Corruption."

"Incoming," says Pig.

"What kind of name is that?" I ask.

Pig jerks his head. I see he means that the bus is coming.

As we pick up all of the drum parts, Denny says, "Remember, slip in the back door. Nobody will notice."

This time it's nearly rush hour. Getting on by the back doors is like swimming upstream to Niagara Falls.

With a drum set. Tired-looking adults glare at us, especially when Denny backs into someone with his drum sticks.

"Hey!" the guy says.

The driver's voice comes on over the intercom. "Boys with the drums, come to the front."

Have you ever tried squeezing down a bus aisle with a bass drum? It's hard to do. I feel like a human bowling ball, but this is not Rock 'N Bowl. I get stuck between a sweaty fat guy with grocery bags and a tall skinny lady who looks away. This is not what being up close and personal with your fans is supposed to mean.

The bus rumbles. I stare at the top of the drum. As we slow for the first stop, Denny squeezes back to me. "We gotta get off," he says. "She says we're creating a disturbance. Besides, I don't have money for a ticket."

I have to back out when the bus stops. I keep my eyes on the drum, but I feel the staring and hear the grumbles. At least we're going with the flow. I make it to the sidewalk before I have to put the drum down. My arms are killing me.

"I bet *they'll* remember us—even without T-shirts," Denny says.

"Incoming," says Pig.

"We just did that," I say. My back is killing me too.

"For a name," Pig says. He doesn't seem tired.

Den is busy tweeting. "I kind of like that," he says. "What about…" Then he forgets to say anything.

We have to walk the rest of the way to my house. At every rest stop, Denny tweets how far we've gone in case any girls want to rush on down to help us. Nobody does.

"Gee, Den," I say, "Maybe you gave the wrong directions."

"Aw, Ace. You watch," Denny says. "Give it one month, and we'll be chick magnets."

"That's how long it's going to take to get to my house," I say.

Denny changes the subject. "I think we should call ourselves The Spank. We could play in jock straps, like the Chili Peppers."

"Spitfires," says Pig.

Denny shakes his head. "That would be like a Kiss cover band. You know, spitting fire? This drum is heavy."

Now Pig shakes his head, but he doesn't say anything. We walk, talking names. Then we stagger, talking names. At least, Denny and I stagger. Pig doesn't even break a sweat.

Pig suggests Surface to Air and Wing Commander or something, and Chopper. I like Chopper. Denny doesn't. Then Pig goes back to Incoming.

I can't think of anything good that isn't taken. Every name I think of reminds me of some other name. By the time we turn down my street, we're back to The Spank or Incoming. Finally, I vote with Pig for Incoming.

"I was just kidding about the jock straps," Denny complains.

"I don't want to get spanked," I say. "I'm not a little kid."

"It's okay," Denny says. "Lots of rock stars are short."

"I'm not short, either," I say. I change the topic. "Incoming, for now."

"It can't be for *now*," Denny says. "We have to start a Myspace page, post pictures, list influences."

He's right. I hate it when Denny's right. I hate carrying a bass drum even more. Luckily, we're at my house.

"Incoming," I say again as I put the drum down on my front step. My fingers stay bent. Archie watches us from the porch.

"Too bad Archie can't take pictures," Denny says. "He could take our first group shot." He drops the snare on the grass. Our lawn isn't much bigger than the drum.

"Hey," says Pig.

"Sorry." Denny lays the other stuff down to tweet again. "Okay, influences?"

Maybe there's blood getting to my brain again. I say, "Nirvana."

"Billy Talent."

"Green Day."

"Chili Peppers."

"Doors."

"Alexisonfire."

"Led Zep."

"Slayer."

"Hendrix," says Denny. His thumbs fly, tweeting. More names come up. It's cool to sit here like real musicians and toss around names of bands we want to sound like.

I imagine our video. I get that image of playing onstage in my head again. I press my fingertips. It's cool that they're sore. Only musicians have sore fingers. And maybe martial-arts guys, from all that eye poking they do. But that would be different. When we stand up again, I'm all stiff. That's cool too. It feels like a sacrifice for my art. I'll blow off some homework and practice again tonight.

Chapter Six

We have our first practice the next afternoon. I discover seven important things about starting a band.

One: *You can't look cool if practice is at your house.*

Denny has spent the whole day carrying his gear around school. I've always made jokes about guys who carry guitars around, but I wish I needed to do it. I know it would make me look way cooler.

Two: *You need all your strings.*

When Denny unpacks his guitar, I say, "Hey, your guitar is missing the high string."

"Oh, yeah. It broke." Denny plugs in. He slips the strap over his shoulder. "Don't worry, I don't use that one much yet anyway. I'm all about the power chords."

He sets his fingers, then jabs at the strings. Out comes a sound like pigs in a blender.

"You got that tuner thingy?" Denny asks.

I hand it to him. I look closer at the head of his guitar. "I thought you said you had a Telecaster."

"I said it was a Tely."

"That says *Teleporter by Thunder* on the head. A Thunder Teleporter? A five-string Thunder Teleporter?"

"So I'll get another string. Anyway, it's a good amp."

The amp says Melodia. It looks like a kindergarten toy.

Three: *Bring earplugs.*

I figure I'm good with tissue, like at Battle of the Bands. Pig pulls on a monster set of noise-blocker head phones.

"What's with those?" I say to him and point.

He pulls a giant padded yellow cup off one ear. "Industrial strength," he says and puts it back on.

Denny finishes tuning his five strings, plugs in and turns up his amp. He tries his power chord again. The top of my head almost comes off. I yell something that not even I can hear. Archie streaks for the stairs.

"Told you it was a good amp," says Denny.

As I dig for more tissue, Pig yells, "Turn up your guitar. I can't hear it."

"What?" yells Denny. "My ears are ringing. I can't hear you."

"What?" Pig hollers as he lifts off a headphone.

"What we all need are earplugs," I say.

"What?" they both yell.

Four: *Don't kiss the microphone.*

Since they can't hear, I lean close to the microphone. Too close. The microphone is also plugged into Denny's amp. There is a shriek louder than the Thunder Teleporter. Upstairs, Archie howls. I pull back and try again.

"What do you want to play?" I ask.

Five: *Your own voice will surprise you.*

I don't hear their answers. Instead I'm thinking, Why does my voice sound whiny and crappy? Do I always sound like that? That can't be me. It must be a cheap mike.

Six: *It's harder than you thought.*

We all look at each other. This is it. We are going to play music. There's a lot of music in the world. Where are we going to start?

It's a no-brainer. We choose "Brain Stew" by Green Day. I've only been playing bass for four days, and I can play it already. You just stay on the top string and work down from the fifth fret. The guitar part is Denny's favorite. It's nothing but power chords, two fingers, max.

"Wait," Denny says, "I'll tweet the world what our very first song is." Out comes the cell.

"Let's go," I say. All at once, I want to play.

Denny finishes. He puts down his phone. We get our fingers ready on the strings. Pig taps on the hi-hat with a stick. "Two, three, four—"

We all start on a different beat.

"Try again," says Denny.

"What?" says Pig.

"Take your headphones off," I yell.

"What?" says Pig.

I scream, *"Take your headphones off. So we can all hear."*

Pig frowns. He keeps the phones around his neck. Denny adjusts the mike. We get ready again.

"Two, three, four—"

Denny and I start on different notes. It's my bad.

"Two, three, four—"

Denny drops his pick. He stands up and bumps the microphone stand. It wobbles toward the amp. There's another feedback scream. I grab the stand and bump the crash cymbal, or is it the ride cymbal? Pig dives over the toms to grab it. I jerk back. There's a crackle and a *gadump* sound as my bass cord pops out.

We settle again. I plug back in.

"Two, three, four—"

This time we get it—for a little while anyway. The first notes of "Brain Stew" fill the room. They're wobbly but loud, and I think they are music. We get through the song twice. Denny's screams are pretty good. Pig has trouble keeping the beat with his feet, but he starts to get it. Even with only five notes to play, I'm not always sure where to fit them with the drums.

The second time through, Denny tries to solo. This is a mistake with only five strings. Oh, well. Pig and I power on.

Seven: *Bring rubber gloves.*

It's not until everything stops and I pull the tissue out of my ears that I hear another sound. It's weird and high, like Robert Plant screaming on a Zep song. Only it's not Robert Plant.

It's Archie yowling and throwing up in the front hall.

"I think we're an extreme band," Denny says.

We are so extreme we make cats barf. I'm cool with that (except for having to clean up), because I love us. Whatever this is that we're doing is the most fun I've ever had.

Chapter Seven

After three more practices we're way better. You can tell because Arch doesn't barf anymore. Sometimes when I take my earplugs out, I hear him yowling upstairs. When I go upstairs to put him outside, he runs right to the door.

I also know we're better because we can blast through "Brain Stew." We can play "Teen Spirit." We're working on playing it backward too. We've started practicing "Seven Nation Army," and we have a list of songs we're going to learn.

Denny now has all six strings. His screaming sounds good, but he doesn't do many stage moves. That's because the basement ceiling is too low.

Pig and I are getting it together too. On "Brain Stew" I match my notes with the bass drum for those two quick beats every time. At first I couldn't figure out when they came in. Then Pig showed me that I could count along to the beat of the hi-hat.

Pig had trouble because he had to make his left hand play every beat on the hi-hat while his right foot played the two fast beats on the drum. See? It's tricky.

Now I'm checking out websites about bass playing. I got some patterns to practice, and I play bass along to our songs on my MP3 player. I've played so much that my fingers hardly ever hurt anymore. My fingertips are all tough and callused, and I can't feel much with them. It turns out it's a good thing I bite my nails too. Guitar and bass players have to keep them short, especially on the left hand. I'm really getting into this, even apart from the girls. Not that I've forgotten that. Chuck said girls can tell musicians by their hands. I hope he's right. I try to keep mine out of my pockets as much as I can.

"Stage two," Denny says while we're walking down the hall at lunch. We're going to eat outside on the bleachers. "We gotta do the Myspace page, and it's gotta have video." He slings his gig bag higher on his shoulder. "My tweeting is already building a fan base. Now they want more."

"How many followers have we *got*, Den?"

"I haven't checked lately. But I know it's for sure more than my mom. So, what we're going to do now"—Denny pulls the door open—"is ask the girls in the video club to help. And I happen to know that they always eat lunch out here."

"*What?*" All at once I'm not hungry. "We can't just ask them. They'll think we're dweebs, that it's a put-on."

I thought girls would gather around after they heard us. I never thought we'd have to ask them to make a video.

Denny shakes his head and says, "No, they won't. Will they, Pig?"

Pig shrugs. "I'll do the Myspace page."

As we cross the football field, I see the girls in the video club sitting in the bleachers. There's Lucy, from grade school, and Jessica from math, and Alison and Nadia. Oh, man. I see hair and smiles and many round body parts.

"Why don't you text them?" I whisper to Denny.

"None of them gave me their numbers," he whispers back.

Great. It's too late now. They see us coming. Are they giggling about us already?

"Hey, Video Club!" Denny calls. Now they're giggling for sure. I can feel myself shrinking.

I look around for Pigpen. He's bigger, and maybe I can duck behind him. He's gone. No, he's sitting by himself way down the bleachers, opening his lunch. How did he do that? There's no time to wonder.

"You guys still looking for a video project?" Denny asks. He's already climbing the bleachers toward the girls.

"Maybe," says Alison. I feel my face turning red, and I shrink some more. The other girls are still giggling.

"Well, me and Ace have got one for you," says Denny. His grin is a mile wide. "You can record our new band. We need performance video for our Myspace page. Have you been reading my tweets?"

More giggling. "We didn't know you were tweeting, Denny." That's Jessica. I love girls with black hair. In fact I love girls of all hair colors. But I have trouble talking to any of them.

Denny babbles on. "We have this new band, Incoming. It's really turning out cool. There's Pigpe...Jared on drums, Ace on bass—hey, that rhymes! And I'm on guitar and lead vocals." Denny spreads his arms out wide. His gig bag bounces. "We promise to rock your worlds!"

Rock your worlds? If I shrink any more, all that will be left of me will be shoes. There's nothing I can do but send beams of *shut up* thoughts at Denny.

51

"Where are you performing?" Lucy asks.

I guess Denny doesn't get my message. He blathers, "Well, nowhere yet. That's why we need a video. To get performances. We just started. We're practicing in Ace's basement."

"In Ace's basement?" says Lucy. I think she's been there, at my sixth birthday party.

"Yeah," Denny says. "Hey, you could put Ace's cat in the video! He barfs every time we play. That's how we know we're extreme." Denny hoists his gig bag. "Or know what, *you could all be in it too!*"

"As what," Nadia says, "adoring fans?"

I wish, but I don't say so. I'd have better luck wishing for death.

Denny says, "Sure! But, no, like, we could make something up. Maybe you could all hate us as much as the cat—"

"You mean we have to barf?" says Jessica.

Denny laughs and says, "No, but, like, we play really badly at first. Then you come in and show us how to rock or something. You know, we could make up a story."

"We'll think about it," Alison says.

"Cool," Denny says. "Let us know soon, okay? We have to get this done, and we want to make it really good." He hops down the steps, the gig bag bouncing on his back. I'm right behind him.

"Okay," they call. There's more giggling.

"And check out my tweets!" he calls.

"Okay!" Now they are laughing.

Halfway across the field I say to Denny, "Nice try." He sounded like an idiot, but I didn't sound like anything, did I?

"Nice try?" Denny says. "Are you kidding? They loved it." Out comes the cell. He tweets: **incoming video 4 sure. Watch 4 it!**

Chapter Eight

"Our time has come," Denny announces at our next practice.

This is news to me. A week has gone by. Girls have not called. Denny's little sister did come over to take pictures. She used Denny's cell phone and shot twenty seconds of video too. Denny tried to play guitar behind his head and bashed out the ceiling light. Pig posted the video and pictures anyway on the Incoming Myspace page. Not all of them show our heads. That could make us a mystery band. He has also printed the words *sonic BOOM!* beside the biggest picture of us on the Myspace page. It's a start anyway.

As I finish tuning my bass I say, "Our time has come? I hope it brought pizza."

"No, really," Denny says. "Look at this."

It's a bright green flyer advertising a contest at the youth center. Everyone can play two original songs, and the winners get to be in a show downtown, right outside City Hall.

"Wait a sec," I say. "Original songs? We don't have original songs. We play covers."

Denny says, "So we'll write some. C'mon, how hard can it be?" He picks up one of the old Razorburn CDs. "These guys did it, right?"

"I guess," I say. "I can't remember."

"Then we can do it too," Denny says. "We can all write together. Listen, I already made up a riff and a first line on the walk here."

Denny plugs in and plays his riff. It's pretty lame. It's a repeat of the same note and then one note down: *duh-duh duh-duh, duh-duh duh-duh*.

"That's it?" I say.

"Listen to the words." He plays again and chants: "Don't wanna be what you call normal." Then he stops. "Okay, what should come next?"

"*That's* it?"

"What do you want?" Denny complains. "It wasn't a long walk. Anyway, we're supposed to write this together."

We jam on Denny's riff. It's not hard to do. Figuring what comes next is hard. We call it "Not So Normal" and get as far as this:

Don't wanna be what you call normal
Be the one who barfs at formals
Be the YouTube booger eater
Be the silent farting tweeter
"Then what?" asks Denny.

"Be the shoe with something on it,"
I say.

"Ewwww," Denny cackles. He really
does cackle "heh-heh-heh" like a dirty
old man. "That's not very mature, Ace."

"Well, maturity is overrated," I say.
"This is a punk song, right?"

"Whoa," Denny says. He hits the
riff: "Ma-tur-it-y is ov-er-ra-ted. Okay,
rhyme that."

Pig says his first word of the
afternoon, "Naked." His nickname fits
his mind anyway.

Denny thinks it over. "It's pretty
close. Does it fit? Dated? Hated?"

I think of a rhyme, but I don't say
it. It's grosser than Pig's suggestion.
Instead, I say, "Let's get some juice."

In the kitchen, Denny is saying, "I told you this would be easy," when I hear the front door. Mom comes in. Archie is trotting ahead of her.

"Hi, guys," she says. "Having practice?"

I nod. She opens the kitchen drawer and pulls out earplugs. Then motormouth Denny blows it, big-time. "Not just having practice," he says. "We're writing a song."

"No kidding," Mom says. "That's great. Davey and I used to have a friend who wrote songs."

"Chuck," says Denny.

Mom smiles and says, "That's right. Did you ever meet him? Anyway, I'd love to hear your song."

Denny's eyes widen into car headlights. Pig starts drinking as if he's dying of thirst. I choke and spray juice out my nose.

Mom isn't exactly our target audience.

"We're just getting started," I say. "We'll play it for you when it's done. C'mon guys, we should get back to work." Our footsteps on the stairs sound like a bad drum roll.

"Not So Normal" doesn't sound so great in a whisper.

"It is a good song," Denny says. "I just don't want to scream it right now. My voice is getting tired." He takes off his guitar.

I have a bad feeling. "Den," I say, turning off my amp, "can you think of one girl you'd dare to sing that song to?"

Denny says, "If I scream enough, nobody will know what—"

"If you scream that much at the contest, no one will know what the words are, and we won't win," I say back.

"Won't win if they *do* know what the words are," says Pig.

He's got a point.

"Well…," says Denny.

I say, "Would you sing it to Nadia, or Lucy or Alison—"

Denny says, "In *Chinese*, maybe. If I knew it."

"Lucy *is* Chinese," I say.

"Japanese," says Pig.

"It doesn't matter," I say. "Those girls are smart. They probably all know Chinese *and* Japanese. Don't duck the question."

"Okay. Probably not," Denny says, as he coils his guitar cord.

I say, "The whole idea was to get girls, right? So we gotta start over."

"But it's hard," Denny complains. He picks up the Razorburn CD again.

I nod at the box of CDs and say, "You said if they could do it, we could too. Maybe we should all try to write a song on our own before our next practice. Then see what we get."

Behind me I hear the zipper on Denny's gig bag. "You want to practice Saturday?" I ask.

"Busy till Saturday night," Pig says. He's pulling on a sweatshirt that says *TOP GUN*. Maybe it's a video game.

I say, "Well, Saturday night?"

Pig nods. I look at Denny. He's already picking up his case. "Yeah, yeah," he says.

I raise my eyebrow and say, "Or will you be busy with Lucy and Jessica and—"

"You'll be the first to know," Denny says.

"In Chinese," I say.

"Later," we all say.

Chapter Nine

Now I have to write a song—and I have a math test tomorrow. Writing and studying get in the way of each other all evening. I decide to take my guitar to school the next morning to get more done on the song after the test. I don't know if I look cool. I'm too busy sweating over the math test and the song to think about being cool. No girls rush me though.

At lunch I look for a quiet place to work on my song. Songwriting is hard, especially with math on the brain. Nearly everything I've thought of sounds like another song or like an equation. It's driving me nuts. I don't want to give up though. I've thought of one little bit, and my future with girls depends on it.

As I walk down the hall, an acoustic guitar jangles from the music room. A high voice is humming. I don't take music at school because I don't want to get stuck playing a dweeb instrument like clarinet. I look inside and see a guy with long red hair and a jean jacket. He's got his back to me, playing a guitar. Is it that guy from No Money Down, maybe? There's an open notebook and a pen on the desk beside him. He stops and writes something.

"Hey," I say, "are you writing a song too?" I'm so into the songwriting that the words just pop out.

He jumps a little and turns. Only he's a she. She has freckles and a tiny green nose stud. She is probably my age. I've never seen her before, but it's a big school.

"Yeah, I am," she says. Her face gets pink. I think mine does too.

I start backing away, saying, "Oh. Sorry. I was just…I'm trying to do one for this contest."

"At Lakeshore Youth Center?" she asks.

"Yeah," I say.

"Me too." She brushes her hair back behind her ear. "What kind of song?"

I clear my throat and say, "Um, a rocker, I guess. I have this pattern."

"Show me," she says. "'Cause right now I'm stuck."

"Really? Wow. Me too." I get out my guitar. "See, this is what I've got so far."

I play a pattern of power chords: 8th fret 3rd 6th 1st. *Duh duh duuh duh-duh*

duh-duh, with the last *duh-duh*s a little faster.

It rocks pretty good. All I need now is a melody and lyrics that you can sing in front of girls. I don't say that out loud.

"What are those chords?" She squints at my hand.

I say, "Um, they're power chords. They come out of the bottom two notes." I carefully make an F barre chord pattern. I hate F chords. They take me forever to make on the guitar and they kill my hand.

"Oh, sweet," she says. "Barre chords, I get. I took acoustic lessons. What frets are you at?"

I show her. She works out that the chords are C, G, B-flat and F.

B-flat and F? Wow. Maybe I'm better than I thought.

She plays them, easily, as barre chords.

I say, "Cool. That's good."

"They sound better with the power chords," she says. "Show me again."

I do. It feels good to show someone else music stuff.

She tries the chords and says, "Cool. I've got to learn those. What comes next?"

I swallow and say, "Ah...uh...that's all I've got. That's why I'm stuck." The room starts to feel too warm.

"Oh," she says. "See, I always start with words." She nods at the desk. "I've got a book full of them. It's the other part that's hard for me. But know what?" She flips her hair behind her ear again. "I don't think you need words there. That part should be your hook or whatever. Then you write a song with that in it."

"Oh." So I haven't written a song yet.

This is bad, but the girl is still talking. "It's in C, right?"

"C?"

"It's in the key of C, right?" she says. "'Cause it starts on C."

"Riiiight." Chuck used to talk about keys. There was something about how chords go together. I'm going to have to find out what they are before this girl finds out I'm a moron. Maybe I should have taken music, clarinets and all.

"So," she says, "after you play that part, try a C again and start singing."

I try it. I don't sing out loud, but I keep that *duh-duh duh-duh* beat going. A word pops into my head: *Running running running*.

Is this an idea? It feels like one. Should I run right now? I don't run. Instead I stop playing and say, "Wow. That really helps."

She smiles and says, "Can I try that power chord again? This right? So that would be G. Then in my song it would be…"

She plays a bouncier rhythm: *bum bum-bum-bum-bum, bum bum-bum-bum-bum*, and goes up the neck and sings:

Hey, when you see me
Don't act so dreamy
Hear every word I say…

Wow. She has a killer voice, and it's a good tune too. She stops. "That sounds way better than this." She plays again, with regular chords.

Now it's my turn to watch hands. I say, "Those are G, A and C, right? Try it again, okay? I can see a bass part." I can't play it that fast right off. "Can you slow down a little?" I ask.

We try it again. This time I can play along. She likes it.

"That is so awesome," she says.

I say, "I'm more of a bass player than a guitarist."

"Really?" she says. "Can you show me again? I want to teach that to our bass player."

I say, "You've got a band? What's it called?"

She says, "No Shirt No Shoes No Service."

Niiiiice.

"We're just getting started," she says.

"Us too," I say. "Mine is called Incoming."

"I like that." She does that hair thing again.

"Who are you into?" I ask.

She starts listing bands. I'm nodding when it really hits me. I'm playing guitar, writing and talking with a super-talented girl who has a killer smile, and, well, a whole lot of other things. *And* she knows tons about music.

She says, "Oh, and Sleater-Kinney too. God, how could I forget?"

Who? I can't ask. I'll look even dumber. Suddenly I'm the Incredible Shrinking Ace again. I say, "Well,

I should probably let you…" I turn to put Chuck's guitar away and clunk it against a desk. "Thanks a lot for helping. That was really…"

"Hey, back at you," she says. "Thanks for showing me power chords and the bass line."

My knees practically melt. There is enough of me left to say, "Um, maybe our bands should do, like, a show together or something. We don't make the cat barf anymore."

She gives her head a shake, as if she hadn't heard right. Then she says, "Awesome." She starts to pack up too. "Bell's gonna go. Hey, Facebook me, okay?"

"Sure." Now I'm trying to fasten the snaps on my guitar case, but my fingers aren't working.

"At Lisa Picks," she says.

"For sure," I say. "I'm Dave. But it'll say, um, Ace. It's, like…"

She nods. "Yeah, a nickname. So's Picks."

"Oh. Yeah. Cool. Well…," I say.

"Yup," says Lisa Picks. "Later."

I'm almost back to my locker when I wonder, Did I tell her we don't make the cat barf anymore? Oh, no. I'm shrinking again.

Chapter Ten

"Ohhh-kay, Ace! Lay it on us." It's Saturday night practice. We've just finished listening to Pig's song. Well, actually it was a drum solo. Archie shot upstairs when Pig got going. I can hear him yowling up there somewhere.

Now it's my turn. My fingers are shaky. I pretend to check my tuning. "Okay," I say, "I'm not quite done yet.

It's, like, a road song." I make the C power chord on the acoustic and blow the start. I take a breath and try again. This time I get it. I don't hit all the high notes, and I mess up a couple of chords, but it's pretty good:

Running running running it's a thing
that I do
Running running running far away
from you
Running running running is the
thing that I know
Running running running and I have
to go
I'm sleeping in the backseat and
running all the time
Duh-duh-duh-duh-duh duh
Duh-duh-duh-duh duh duh
Duh.

I stop. "The *duh*s aren't really the lyrics. I haven't got them right yet. But that's the idea."

It's still quiet. I say, "And I didn't hit all the high notes 'cause…" I point upstairs, where Mom might be listening.

It's *still* quiet. Finally, Denny nods and says, "Okay." Pig shrugs and nods.

That's all that they say. I feel like Led Zeppelin with a leak. Geez, all Pig came up with was a drum solo. *A drum solo.* I only said I liked it to be nice.

"It's okay? That's it?" I hear my voice squeak a little.

"Well, what do you want?" Denny says. "We only heard it once."

What do I want? I was hoping for fireworks and these guys falling off their chairs. Then a standing O, a million dollars and Lisa forgetting the cat barf comment and saying I'm cool.

"Want me to play it again?" I say.

"Let me do mine first." Denny grins and pulls out a distortion pedal. "Wait till you hear this," he says. He plugs the Teleporter into it and hits a power chord. The sound crunches through the basement.

"Okay," Denny says. He unfolds a paper with writing on it and lays it on his amp. "This is called 'Got to Rock.'"

"That's original," I say. I fold my arms tight. My pits have gone cold where I've been sweating.

Denny doesn't seem to hear. He starts chopping a rhythm so fast it's practically punk. He sings:

Used to walk but now I run
Used to talk but now it's sung
Used to dock—now I roam
Used to sway but now I rock
Used to groove but now I shock
Got to rock—like a rolling stone

He gets that far, and I already know it's good. It's way better than mine. Even though we're all a band, I feel like I'm doomed. Halfway through, Mom sprouts magically on the stairs.

When Denny finishes, she claps. Then she takes out an earplug and asks, "Is that one that you guys wrote?"

"Well, I did, actually," Denny says. He's grinning like a maniac. "It's for the contest." He tells my mom all about it.

"Wow," says Mom. "That's great. It's catchy. It reminds me of...oh, I don't know, what's that song? What is it, Davey?"

I shrug and I say, "I'm not an Abba expert." My mom loves Denny's song. This does not make me overjoyed.

Denny jumps in, saying, "It sounds a little like lots of songs, probably. That's how you can tell it's good."

Thank you, Mr. Modest.

"I never thought of it that way," Mom says. "You said two songs. What's the other?"

"Ace wrote one," Denny says.

"Later," I say to Mom. I start to fold up my paper.

"Oh, c'mon." she says.

"Later."

Mom shakes her head. "Then later it will be," she says. "Does anyone want anything to drink?"

"A pitcher of draft, please," Denny says.

"Dream on, Denny." Mom laughs and heads for the stairs. "I'll bring down some juice for all of you," she says over her shoulder.

Sunday afternoon, Mom goes to an open house for real estate agents. I promise to do homework. She's happy because I got a B on my math test. (Okay, it was B minus, but it still counts.)

I really do homework, because I can't face music. I know it's wrong, but it bugs me that Denny's song is better than mine, even if it gives us a shot at the contest. How did the guy do it?

I guess there's no reason he couldn't. Except that it's Denny. That means I'm jealous. Of Denny. I never thought I'd be jealous of Denny.

Finally I ditch homework and practice my song. We do get to do two songs for the contest, and my song is better than a drum solo. I sing it again. I hate my voice. Then I have a really bad thought. Lisa is going to like Denny's song better than mine. Oh man, Denny's going to be all over her.

I haven't told Denny about Lisa. I found her on Facebook and sent a friend request. I'd imagined playing my song to her in the music room and her loving it. And me. Now I don't think I want to.

What I have to do is make my song better—except I don't know how. How can Denny write like that when I can't? I sing mine again. I still hate my voice.

I can't help it; I check Denny's Twitter feed: **dr. D writes monster incoming hit 4uall sensstionel.**

I can feel my teeth grind. To get my mind off it, I hunt around for some music to play to. I've left my MP3 player at school. Darn. There aren't many CDs around the house. Mom's are awful.

Then I remember Chuck's. I haven't listened to it in a million years. I go downstairs and grab one from the box. I'm using Chuck's gear, so he won't mind if I listen to his album too.

The front cover says *RAZORBURN: Mullet Over.*

The picture shows a guy's head and back, with a long blond mullet hanging down under a straw cowboy hat. The back of the CD shows the same guy without the hat. He is bald on top. That was Chuck for you. Liked his hats. Usually wore his hair back in a ponytail.

I peel off the shrink wrap and pop the CD in the player. The first two tunes are yawner country rock. We must have listened to this when Chuck was around, but I don't remember these songs at all.

I play along a little. They're boring but easy. I'm getting better at guessing what chords go together. Hey, that means I'm learning my keys. That makes me feel a little better. I skip ahead. The third tune is a horrible ballad. The fourth is more pop. It has a guitar riff that's okay, and the intro sounds familiar. Maybe Chuck used to play it. The singer starts in:

Used to run, but now I walk
Used to sing, but now I talk
Used to dock...

Wait a minute.

Used to rock but now I sway
Used to gleam but now I fade...

It sounds *very* familiar. And all at once I know how Denny did it.

Chapter Eleven

It's lunchtime on Monday before I see Denny. I've been stewing about the song rip-off the whole time. I don't say anything while we eat, because other kids sit with us. Besides, Denny is blabbing a mile a minute about the video club girls. Then we all start playing Frisbee. One by one the other guys leave, and there's only Denny and me left. I can't take it any longer.

I've planned it to casually say, "I listened to Chuck's CD yesterday," but now I'm too mad from waiting.

What comes out is, "You stole the song." Then I throw the Frisbee back to Denny. Hard.

"No, I didn't," Denny insists. "Not exactly. Ow!" He shakes his hand and throws back too high.

I jump for it and miss. I walk to get it. I'm not running for Denny. I turn around and say, "You changed the words around and sped it up. Big deal. It's still a rip-off. And you stole one of Chuck's CDs."

Denny laughs. "Oh, come on, Ace. I borrowed it. You can have it back."

I throw the Frisbee back to him, harder. Now I'm almost yelling. "That's not what matters, and you know it. No wonder your song was so good. You cheated. I really wrote a song."

"Hey, not so loud, okay?" Denny says and looks around.

I snap, "What? Are you afraid the video girls might hear?"

"Yeah," he says. His throw goes high again. I have to jump for it. "I've been hanging with them. They're getting interested in a project."

"Right," I say. I throw too low.

"No, they are. Who knows what might happen?" Denny wiggles his eyebrows. He throws high *again*. I jump to my right and miss.

"Don't change the subject. You copped the song. I wrote one."

Denny sighs and says, "Look, Ace, no offence but, which one was better? Huh? I don't mean your song sucks. There isn't time to write a *good* song. The contest is next Friday." He throws. This one I catch, even though it's way over my head.

Denny is as crappy at Frisbee as I am. I'm surprised he doesn't have someone throwing for him. I throw back another worm burner.

"We're going to do your song too," Denny says.

I moan. "Aw, for—"

"My bad," Denny says.

Denny's throw has gone really wild this time. The Frisbee is hanging from a tree branch. We jump for it, but it's just out of reach. We're not supposed to climb the trees at school, but this one is easy and it'll take a second. I start for it, but Denny scrambles up first. He reaches for the branch.

"Look, Ace," he says from above, "we're in this together, right? It doesn't matter who *wrote* the song, as long as it's ours, right? And we're all working to learn how to play it, right? So we're all kind of writing it. With Chuck. We're getting his song heard, and we're making it better. It's not like we're ripping him off for money."

I don't say anything.

"We don't have to say it's mine," Denny says. "It's ours. Okay?"

I look up at Denny. He's got his big goofy grin on his face. "We want to win, right? Video club girls, right?"

I think about winning. Forget the video club girls. I imagine Lisa thinking that I helped write the song.

I nod. Denny shakes the tree branch. The Frisbee drops into my hand like a big fat apple. I look up. Denny's already tweeting.

Chapter Twelve

I get to be Facebook friends with Lisa. It's stupid, but I am too chicken to ask if she wants to meet up at lunch one day. I tell myself she's too busy anyway, that her band is probably practicing. I'll see her at the contest.

The contest is coming up fast. We're supposed to be practicing too, but really I am the only one who practices.

Pig is "busy." With what? Who knows? His hair is even shorter, and now he wears aviator shades all the time. Denny, Mister Showbiz, is too busy tweeting. All he ever talks about is Alison and Jessica and the other video girls. He's late all the time. Do they care about this, or what?

Meanwhile, I keep working on my song. I mean, how cool would it be if mine got so good that *it* won? Then it wouldn't matter about Chuck's song. I get all the *duhs* out of my lyrics. I decide to call it "Sleeping in the Backseat."

I like my tune so much that I'm almost okay with playing it for Mom. I don't want to tell her that though. Instead I strum Chuck's guitar a bunch when she's around, in case that gives her the idea to ask about my song.

I'm playing guitar in the kitchen on Tuesday when she comes in. She's carrying red flowers—roses I think.

She's all cheery and fussing around, cutting the stems and putting water in a vase.

"There's another math test next week," I tell her. *Strum, strum.*

"Well, I'm sure you'll do fine," Mom says. She puts the vase on the kitchen table and starts to stick the flowers in it.

I say, "Yeah, can't start studying till after the contest though." *Strum, strum, strum.*

"Mm," says Mom. "Is that on Friday? Oh, darn. I hope I don't have to present an offer on a house that night." She doesn't sound very upset. I'm not sure how I feel about that.

I play some more, running through my chord changes. "Well," I say, "guess I should go practice…" *Strum, strum.*

"Okay, sweetie." Mom kisses me on the top of the head. Then she flips open her cell phone. "Just have to check my messages, then we'll talk about dinner."

She heads off to the living room, smiling like summer holidays started. I guess the real estate market is looking up.

I go to the basement and sing "Sleeping in the Backseat" loud enough for Mom to hear. When I finish, I hear her laughing and talking on her phone. Rats. I thought being a songwriter would make me a chick magnet, but right now not even my mom is listening.

Even worse, Denny and Pig haven't heard my tune lately either. They don't know how I've changed it. When we finally practice on Wednesday, Denny keeps messing up the new lyrics. He puts the stupid *duh*s back in instead.

"I'll sing it myself," I tell him as we pack up.

"No sweat," Denny says. I'm surprised. Denny likes being the lead singer. He likes being lead everything. "What we really gotta decide,"

Denny goes on, "is what we're going to wear on Friday. I'm going grunge, but with style."

I say, "Such as?"

"New Converse," Denny says. "What are you wearing, Pig?"

Pig shrugs. He's been unscrewing cymbals and stacking them neatly to take with us to the contest. Now he unzips his backpack and puts his drumsticks in. I have to look twice. His textbooks in there are each covered in plastic. Finally Pig says, "What I'm wearing." He's wearing a T-shirt that says *Cleared For Takeoff*. I hope we are.

"I'm going dark," I say. I decide to go with my acid-wash jeans and the tight dark blue shirt. I think dark blue goes with bass. It'll make me look like a serious musician. I'm not going to shave, either. You can tell now when

I don't, kind of, right on my chin. I rub my chin right now. It feels a little prickly. Or maybe it's all of me that's feeling prickly. Thinking about Friday is making me nervous.

Chapter Thirteen

Friday night Pig's dad gives us a ride to the youth center. We have to haul amps and cymbals and the snare and foot pedal for the drum kit, plus the guitars. Pig's dad doesn't talk any more than Pig does.

"There will be beautiful women watching. I know there will be beautiful women." Denny's motormouth is in overdrive. He must be nervous. Plus he's texting or tweeting or something.

Pig's dad laughs. I say, "Yes, Den. And they'll all be watching you." By now my right foot is bouncing like my own rhythm section, and I've got elevator stomach. I'm thinking about a million things at once. Will we win? Will Lisa love my song? Will Lisa love me? Does getting a ride from someone's dad counts as a road trip? It has to count more than moving drums on the bus.

The youth center hasn't changed much. I used to go there to play floor hockey when I was little. The first thing I see is lots of guys in dark blue shirts. Darn. There are parents here too. Luckily, Mom has to present that offer on a house. That's one less thing to worry about.

We haul everything into the gym. It's set up with a low stage with mikes and stands and a drum kit that looks as if it has been attacked by gorillas. A spotlight shines down. The Twisted Hazard guys from Battle of the Bands are setting up.

My elevator stomach jumps twenty floors. We're really going to do this.

I see more kids from Battle of the Bands, but it's Lisa I'm looking for. Then I spot her. She's across the gym, behind another girl and three guys. They seem to be all talking at the same time. I wave, but I don't think she sees me. That's okay. She's busy. I'm busy too— busy being nervous.

We sign in at the judge's table. We are going to be on fifth, out of ten acts. Is that good or bad? I don't know. Denny keeps asking what time they think we'll be on. I don't care about that. "What number is No Shirt No Shoes No Service?" I ask.

"They're right before you," says a bald guy who is one of the judges.

We go to tune up. It feels good to have something to do.

Twisted Hazard kicks off. It's hard to tell about their songs. They pretty much all sound the same, especially with earplugs in. One song is either about *macaroni* or *mayday homey*. But it's not rap, so *homey* doesn't make sense. Macaroni? Who knows. They're loud and they rock though. I look at the judges. They're writing stuff down. Is that good or bad?

The second band is called Death Star. They're pure metal, sort of like Iron Maiden but dumb. One song has the word *troll* in it a lot, and the other is something about hammers. The judges write more stuff down. They can't like troll songs, can they?

Third come two guys with acoustic guitars. I don't catch their names. They play exactly the same thing and take turns singing about a magic potion. They sing so high they squeak.

I'm starting to feel better. I know "Sleeping in the Backseat" is better than these.

Now No Shirt No Shoes No Service is up. I know Lisa's song is good. If we don't win, I want her band to win and us to come in second.

"Let's tune again," Denny says. He's looking at his watch. Then he looks all around. "Beautiful women, beautiful women," he keeps saying. Pig is drumming the wall. He's got his aviator shades on. How can he see anything?

"In a minute," I say. I push forward. A guy is plugging in a keyboard. The other girl is the drummer. There's a guy on bass, and Lisa and the other guy on acoustics. Lisa looks incredible. She's got on soft boots and leggings and this short skirt with her jean jacket. The little green stone in her nose catches the light. She pulls the mike down to her level and looks out at the crowd in front of the stage.

I hope she sees me. I don't want to do anything dorky like wave. She looks my way, and I think she recognizes me. Just then the guitar guy counts, "Two… three…" and they start.

Hey, when you see me
Don't act so dreamy…

But Lisa's song has gone from being a cool indie rocker to a drippy emo ballad. The power chords are gone. The drummer loses a beat. The guy on keyboard messes up a wimpy solo. The bass player uses one string, and none of the bits I showed Lisa. Lisa's voice wobbles with the slow time.

I hang in long enough to clap at the end of the tune. Lisa doesn't look happy. I head back to get my bass.

"They suck," Denny says. He's bouncing on his toes. He has his Teleporter slung on. Pig is still drumming the wall.

Denny's right, but I don't want to say it. "It's a good song though," I say.

"Ours is better," Denny says.

"Ours *are* better," I snap. "Tell me about it." I plug my bass into the tuner as their second song begins. I may sound okay, but my fingers are shaking. Tuning seems to take forever. I slip the bass strap over my head. The patch cord is coiled in my hand. Now I hear clapping as Lisa's band finishes. They announce that Incoming is next.

"Let's do it," says Denny. I follow him and Pig. I almost stumble on the one step to the stage. The amp is heavy. The lights are hot. It takes me two tries to plug in. Then I turn and look out from the stage.

I have to squint in the glare. Pig's shades suddenly seem like a good idea. This may be the youth center, but it feels like Madison Square Gardens. There are a lot of people here. There is also a microphone right in front of me. I'd swallow but there's nothing to swallow. My elevator stomach lurches into a free fall.

Behind me, I hear Pig setting up. He rumbles around the kit and moves something. I fumble out a couple of bass notes. Denny is messing with his distortion pedal. Now he smacks a test chord. From out front there is a buzz of voices. I look at Denny. He's grinning like he lives on a stage. I start to feel it too. We're a team. I *want* this. Maybe I've been waiting for this my whole life and not known it. My stomach stops before the basement. I take a deep breath and run a few more notes on my bass. Pig is still fussing. Now Denny's waving. I look to the back, and coming in the doors are Alison and Lucy from the video club, then Jessica with a camera up in front of her. What the…?

There isn't time to wonder. The judges nod for us to start. As Pig counts us in, I see the girls shuffle forward. Two more people squeeze in behind them. One of them is Mom. She's with a guy, arm in arm. The guy has a mustache and one of those stupid old-guy western-style hats, a long leather jacket and dad jeans. I've seen him before. As we come in on the first beat, I remember where. My place. A long time ago. It's Chuck.

Chapter Fourteen

We rock out. Pig nails the beat. Denny half sings and half screams, and it works. He also bounces, jumps, drops to his knees and flicks a pick out into the crowd. He even plays okay. Lucy and Alison and Jessica are right down in front, filming.

And I hate every second of it. I pretend I have to watch my fingers.

I don't look up once. There's lots of clapping when we finish. Denny does a big goofy bow and before I can stop him, says, "Thanks. We all wrote that, from my idea."

I have to look. Chuck has his dumb hat pushed up on his bald head. He's got his arms crossed, and he's talking to Mom.

Now he's looking at me, standing onstage with his bass beside the guy who just claimed we wrote Chuck's song. It was supposed to be Chuck who had reliability issues.

I know what I have to do. Before Denny can say anything else, I step to my microphone. "Uuuh," I say.

I've stepped too close, and what they hear is *UUUUH* with a huge squeal of feedback. The whole room jumps, including me.

"Uh," I try again. "Uh, actually, there's another writer." My voice sounds like a strangled chicken. Heads lift at the judge's table. I'm not going to look at Denny. I squint at the far basketball hoop. "Our friend Chuck wrote it. He let us change it around and that helped us get started." I point. "He's back there."

Heads turn. Chuck grins and waves. There is more clapping. "He loaned me his bass too," I say. The clapping is still going on. "So, anyway, I don't know if that counts, but we did write this one by ourselves."

I look at the judge's table. This time they're not writing, they're scratching lines right across their papers. Oh, no. I can't look at Denny. I'm not even looking at the basketball hoop now. My eyes are closed. I clutch my bass and play the opening of "Sleeping in the Backseat."

I know I've got the beat wrong even before I sing the first line. Pig and I get out of time. Denny hits a wrong chord and forgets to sing on the chorus.

While we mangle my song, part of me floats above everything. That part of me is calm. It wonders what sounds worse than a strangled chicken. Archie barfing? A sick ostrich? Pick one, it tells the rest of me, because that's how you sound, especially on that high note you can never quite reach—the one that's coming up *now*. Then it tells me that "Sleeping in the Backseat" still sucks. All that *running, running, running* doesn't cut it. Meanwhile, the rest of me feels as if I'm in a train wreck.

There's a trickle of clapping when we finish. Then comes the kiss of death.

Someone at the back is clapping like crazy. I don't even have to look to know it's Mom.

Chapter Fifteen

As we come offstage I know one thing. Now that I've blabbed that we didn't write our good song, no one's going to listen to us again. Ever. Actually I know two things, because I also know that I feel so crappy I don't want to see anybody. Too bad that's not an option. Mom and Chuck are already in front of me.

"Hon, I *loved* it! Why didn't you play that for me before? It's so *sensitive*."

"Thanks, Mom."

Mom laughs. "Don't be sarcastic, you. I had to shuffle a lot of things, but I wouldn't have missed that for the world." Then she says, "And look who I met at an agent's open house last week!"

"Davey," Chuck says, "how are ya?" Chuck is grinning. He sticks out his hand. Mine are full. He sees and laughs. "Know the feeling." His mustache is shorter now. He's thicker-looking. "Man," he says. "Did that take me back! Who'd have thought you guys would still be listening to that stuff? Loved what ya did with it! Make me a million, okay? Hey, we've got to do some pickin'. You still got the guitar too?"

I nod.

"Smokin'," says Chuck. "You're on! Haven't played since I gave up truckin'.

Sell houses now like your mom. I'll be over, okay? Let's do it."

I nod again. I'm still trying to catch up. Mom takes Chuck by his leather-coated arm and says, "We're going to grab a quick bite, hon. Do you want to come with us?"

"I'd better stay here," I say.

Mom smiles and says, "All right. We won't be late."

Next it's Denny and Pig. I see them at the guitar cases. I'm still thinking about my mom's "*We* won't be late." Denny and Pig won't look at me. I know I have to say it.

I put down the bass amp. It's killing my arm. "Look," I say, "sorry, but I saw them come in. I had to."

"Aw, no sweat." Denny shrugs as he snaps his case shut. "Alison said they got good footage."

That makes me feel a little better. After all, it's not as if the whole world was here. "So Pig can post it on Myspace," I say.

"Well," Denny stands and shuffles. Then he says, "It wasn't exactly for that. See, they were just filming me. For a video club project."

"Video club?" I say.

Denny says, "Yeah, I joined, 'cause like, the girls wanted me too. We're making this movie." Denny shrugs and makes a face. He says, "So, like, sorry, Ace, but I have to bail on the band. There's not gonna be enough time for music."

"But—," I say.

"Me too," says Pig, from behind his shades. It might be the first thing he's said all night.

"What?" I spin to him. "You joined video club too?"

"No," Pig says. "I'm in air cadets. Always was."

"*Air cadets*?" I say.

Pig nods and points to his *Cleared For Takeoff* T-shirt. "I'm starting flying lessons," he says.

Suddenly the boots and the hair and the shades make sense. Pig says, "And my brother wants his drums at school anyway." He hoists the snare and cymbals.

"But," I say again, "but…"

It's over. Just like that. Incoming is outgoing.

Pig doesn't stay to watch the rest of the bands. He has cadet training camp early Saturday morning. Denny goes to find the video girls. He says I should come too. I shake my head and put my bass away. There are no props this time.

The next band isn't even finished, and my band is done for good. I have had the shortest music career ever. All that's left is jamming with a bald real estate agent who wears dumb hats and redates my mom.

I sink down by my case and lean against the wall. Music bounces around me, but I don't take it in. I'm staring at the floor tiles when I see the toes of two soft boots. Oh. No. It's the person I least want to see after I've looked like a total idiot.

Lisa sits down beside me. "Hi," she says.

"Hi." I nod to the stage and say, "They're good." As if I'm listening.

Lisa says, "Yeah. We weren't. We sucked."

"Tell me about it," I say back, and shrug. "At least—never mind. I liked your song."

"Thanks," she says.

I wait for her to say she liked mine, but she doesn't.

After a bit I say, "How come you changed your song? I liked it better as a rocker." I did, but I guess I'm also bugged she didn't say anything about my song.

"I did too," she says. "But the band wanted to do it that way. And Grant couldn't play the bass line you showed me."

"That's a drag," I say.

Lisa nods. "Same with yours," she says. "No offence, but your guitar player should have sung, and you could have rocked out on bass."

I nod. "Well," I say, "he didn't learn it, so I had to do it. It doesn't matter. I know I've gotta change the words more. It's still not very good." I wrap my arms around my knees. "And anyway, it *really* doesn't matter. The band just broke up."

Lisa nods and says, "Mine too."

I look at her. "Your band broke up? Why?"

She sighs, then tucks her hair behind her ear and says, "'Cause we sucked and I said so, and nobody but me wanted to practice more so we wouldn't suck."

I think that over as a song ends. Maybe it's my night for saying things. I look at Lisa. Then I look a little bit to one side of her, as if I'm thinking deep thoughts. "We've got guitar, vocal and bass," I say. Deep breath. "Um, maybe we should start a band."

I dare a look at her.

She's smiling. Lisa says, "I think we just did."

Since the publication of his first picturebook, *Puddleman*, in 1988, Ted Staunton has been delighting readers of all ages with his funny and perceptive stories about friends, family and school life. Ted is a frequent speaker and performer at schools, libraries and conferences across Canada and teaches fiction writing at George Brown College. Ted and his family live in Port Hope, Ontario.

orca currents

9781554694341 $9.95 PB
9781554698882 $16.95 LIB

In most ways, Poe is like the other kids in his school. He thinks about girls and tries to avoid teachers. He hangs out at the coffee shop with his best friend after school. He has a loving father who helps him with his homework. But Poe has a secret, and almost every day some small act threatens to expose him.

orca *currents*

9781554699100 9.95 PB
9781554699117 16.95 LIB

Fifteen-year-old Maddie has big-city dreams, and she's found her chance to visit New York. An art magazine is holding a portrait contest, and the first prize is an all-expenses-paid trip to the Big Apple. Maddie plans to win, but her mother has different ideas for her: a mother-daughter adventure in organic gardening. Maddie is furious. How will she find an inspiring subject for her portrait amid the goat poop and chickens?

orca *currents*

9781554698202 $9.95 PB
9781554698219 $16.95 LIB

Suspended from school, lonely and bored, fifteen-year-old Zack will do anything for amusement. His mom drags him out geocaching, and Zack finds a CD with the word *Famous* written across it. He puts the CD on his stereo and loses himself in the music. Zack has sound-color synesthesia. He sees colors when he hears music, and the music on the *Famous* CD causes incredible patterns of color for him. Zack becomes obsessed with the girl on the CD and decides he has to find her.

Titles in the Series

orca currents

music / Art

(and plagiarism!)